big & SMALL

Original Korean text by Sang-wu Shim
Illustrations by Ji-ye Jeong
Korean edition © Yeowon Media Co., Ltd.

This English edition published by Big & Small in 2015
by arrangement with Yeowon Media Co., Ltd.
English text edited by Joy Cowley
English edition © Big & Small 2015

Distributed in the United States and Canada by
Lerner Publishing Group, Inc.
241 First Avenue North
Minneapolis, MN 55401 U.S.A.
www.lernerbooks.com

ISBN: 978-1-925186-11-6

Printed in the United States of America

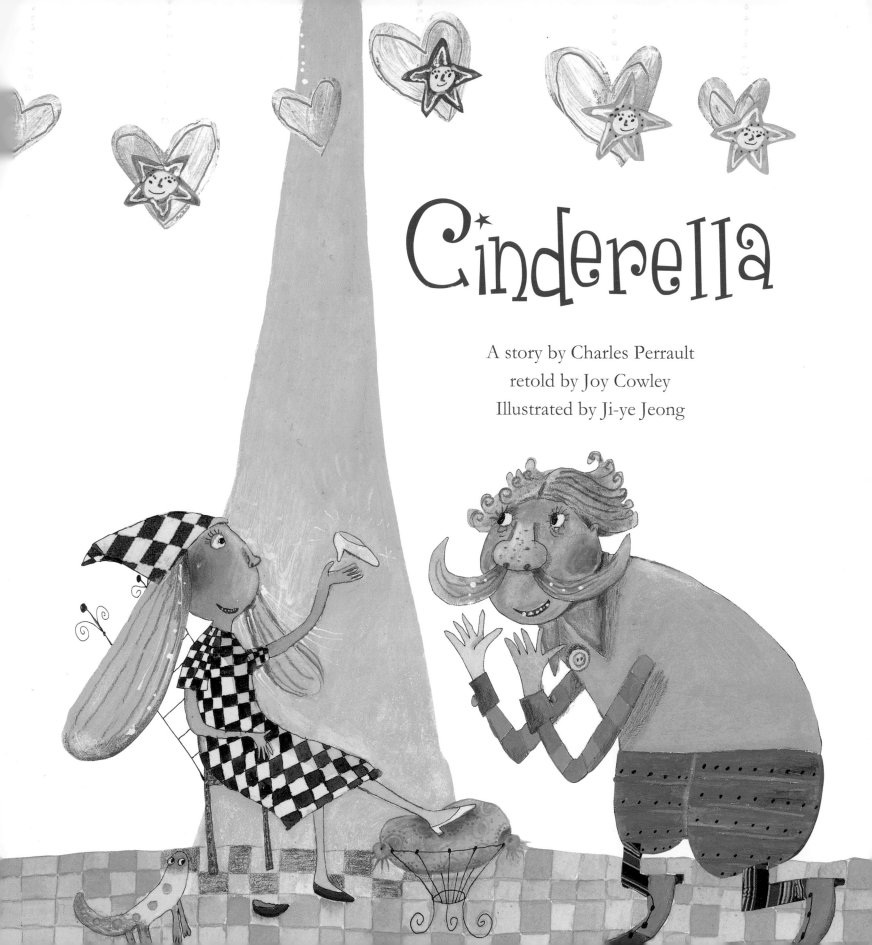

Cinderella

A story by Charles Perrault

retold by Joy Cowley

Illustrated by Ji-ye Jeong

Once there was a kind little girl,
whose mother had died.
Her father married again
and the girl lived with her stepmother.

The stepmother had two daughters
who were older than the girl.
They were bad-tempered and wicked
and they were envious
because the girl was pretty.

Unfortunately, her father
died too, and the girl was left to the care
of her stepmother and her daughters,
who were very mean to her.

The girl had to sleep in the attic.
During the day she did all of the housework:
preparing meals, washing clothes,
scrubbing floors and collecting wood.
All that she had to eat
were scraps of food left over
from her stepsisters' plates.

Because her clothes were rags
and smudged with ash from the fire,
her stepsisters called her Cinderella.

They sang, "Cinderella! Ash on your face.
Hurry up and clean this place."

One day there was an invitation
to a royal ball at the palace.
Cinderella helped her stepsisters dress.

She brushed her stepmother's hair
and helped her with her make-up.
Then she watched them leave for the ball.

Cinderella was all alone and crying
when her fairy godmother came.
"Cinderella," her fairy godmother said.
"Do you want to go to the ball?
I can help you. Bring me a pumpkin,
two mice and a lizard."

15

The fairy godmother changed the pumpkin into a beautiful golden carriage. The two mice turned into horses, and the lizard became a coachman.

Cinderella's ragged clothes
became a sparkling ball gown.
Two shiny glass slippers
were put on her feet.

As Cinderella got in her coach,
her fairy godmother said,
"You must be home by midnight.
Everything will turn back to what it was
when the clock strikes twelve."

"I promise," said Cinderella,
and the coach left for the palace.

When Cinderella arrived at the ball,
the prince fell in love with her.
He did not look at anyone else.
He danced only with Cinderella.

"She is so beautiful," people said.
"Who is she? Where does she come from?"
The stepmother and stepsisters
did not recognize Cinderella,
but they looked at her with envy.

Cinderella was so happy with the prince
that she did not notice the time.
She was shocked when the palace clock
chimed the twelve strokes of midnight.
"I must hurry home!" she told herself.
"The magic spell will soon be broken."
In her hurry to run away from the palace,
one of her glass shoes came off.

The prince picked up the glass shoe.
He said to his servant, "I will marry
the lady who fits this shoe."

The servant arrived at Cinderella's house.
"Give that shoe to me," said a stepsister.
"That is my shoe and I will marry the prince."

"No!" said the other stepsister. "It is mine."
But although they tried and tried,
they could not fit their feet into the shoe.

The servant said to them.
"Is there anyone else in this house?"

"No," said her stepmother.
"Only my two daughters."

Cinderella had been watching.
"May I try it on?" she said.

"Not her!" cried her stepmother.
"She is only our maid."

Cinderella tried on the glass shoe.
It fitted her perfectly.
She took the other glass shoe
from her pocket, and put it on.

Her stepmother and stepsisters
realized that she was the one
who had danced with the prince.
They screamed with fury.

Soon after,
Cinderella married the prince.
They were very happy
and Cinderella was known
for her beauty and kindness.

She was so kind, that she took care
of her stepsisters and stepmother
for the rest of their lives.